art: MIKE DUBISCH   publisher: ODDNESS   editor: CODY GOODFELLOW

FORBIDDEN FUTURES 2

ISBN: 9781960213075 (v3)

LOVECRAFT MEANS NEVER HAVING TO SAY YOU'RE SORRY
CODY GOODFELLOW

THE LATEST LOVECRAFTIAN MORAL CRISIS/TEACHABLE MOMENT has peaked and rolled back under the weight of countless other cultural controversies, but it's useful to reflect on it in anticipation of the next time we have the same fight, and perhaps to get some of those still staring daggers at each other across an arbitrary scrimmage line to recognize their real, common enemies.

For a while, it looked as if HPL was going to get his proper respect. With a Library of America collection curated by Peter Straub and a run of Penguin editions edited by HPL biographer S.T. Joshi, Lovecraft was poised last decade to take his place alongside Poe as a defining force of modern American letters. The archetypal cult author, Lovecraft was already the wellspring of a thriving underground sub-genre, the face of the prestigious World Fantasy Award (by way of Gahan Wilson) and an icon for weirdos everywhere; but at long last, it looked as if he'd finally become an accepted staple of the American canon. But then he walked into a conspiracy of critical and social media buzzsaws that has left the previously radically inclusive cult of Cthulhu in a state of perpetual internecine warfare. After a rocky debate, the World Fantasy Award now looks like the bonsai tree logo for Mr. Miyagi's karate dojo, and Lovecraft has been banished back to the hinterlands of cult obscurity.

Staunch HPL fanatics largely forfeited the debate by falling back on the same dismissive rhetoric that had served in the past. HPL's racism was a product of his times, which still tolerated Jim Crow and saw African natives on exhibit alongside primates in many zoos. HPL's racism was a byproduct of his cloistered, abusive upbringing and penurious, degrading failures in adulthood; but he was beginning to evolve and might well have become a progressive had he lived long enough. He (eventually) rebuked Hitler! He traveled to Florida (once)! Lovecraft was a gentle soul who never uttered an unkind word in public. And most of all, Lovecraft's racism was written off as largely irrelevant, given the plurality of Lovecraft fans he probably wouldn't have wanted to share a cab with.

Weak sauce indeed, and offered under duress, with the impatient disingenuousness of not wanting to have the argument at all. Many Lovecraftians who never faced charges of racism were confronted with parsing that separating the artist from the art is a trick only possible for white magicians, and were not up to the task.

Lovecraft's racism was as extraordinary as his prose, and inseparable from his fiction. However difficult was his life experience, dumber, more deprived folks than himself had awakened to the intellectual cancer of racism and evolved past it in considerably fewer than forty-six years. And while he never called anyone nigger or kike to their face or participated in an Alabama cross-burning, he exhaustively promoted his overtly racist views in amateur editorials, letters and much of his fiction, giving aid and comfort to more tangibly racist readers.

A few unapologetically reactionary critics like Robert Price have burned bridges in the community by embracing Lovecraft's xenophobic rhetoric, in chilling resonance with the nativist hate-mongers of the modern alt-right. But if the majority of Lovecraft's fans were not themselves racists (and I will bet my tentacle miter that the bulk of us land solidly in progressive political turf), they simply didn't want to be reminded of Lovecraft's racism, or to acknowledge the privileged position of being able to take innocent pleasure in tainted art. What does it matter if Lovecraft was racist? We're not… (Are we?)

Without endorsing any of his political beliefs, HPL's self-appointed champion S.T. Joshi has famously short-circuited critical debate on Lovecraft's racism by famously dividing the weird horror community into loyal purists and "Lovecraft haters," vilifying the work and sensibilities of all who find fault with the sage of Providence's blinkered worldview. The resulting circular firing squad has left many reasonable weird fiction fans checking out in disgust.

As we struggle to evolve towards a more inclusive society and yet see forces of divisiveness redefining our nation plodding towards corporatist dystopia, we are experiencing genuine cosmic horror, true existential angst. The fear of being erased, of being trapped in an inimical, mindless universe, is all too fucking real. If corporations are people, then people are not even amoebas, according to the new discourse. Safer, cleaner and more entertained than ever, yet somehow the modern world sucks like never before. So it becomes all the more essential for our fantasies to reflect our ideals and speak more respectfully to a wider audience. When you have to suffer racists and sexual predators to harangue you from the White House, why let them colonize your imagination, too?

Why indeed, but to dismiss cosmic horror as fantasy misses a cardinal point in the complex and problematic Lovecraft issue. If we define fantasy as escape into an impossible dream, Lovecraft's oeuvre is almost anti-fantasy. Even his early Dreamlands fantasies are mired in the poignant irony of the disparity between awe-inspiring dreams and shitty waking life. And his Cthulhu Mythos is the ultimate anti-fantasy, the crushing blow not only to dreams of individual derring-do, but of the effectuality of the entire species, the whole empty, meaningless game. In tone, it is closer to the morbid pessimism of Kafka, Celine and Sartre (to whom Colin Wilson, in a caustic biographical entry on HPL, compared Lovecraft, whom he also called "sick" and a "bad writer," despite a pernicious lasting influence on his own work), than to any other fantasist, and closer to fantasy or science fiction, than any horror writer.

As Michel Houllebecq so astutely points out in Lovecraft: Against The World, Against Life, Lovecraft's racism was a mainspring of his fiction, but it was only the banal face of his greater, raging misanthropy. Seen even in the context of all literature as a rejection of waking, consensus reality, Lovecraft's fiction is a particularly bitter pill that reduces humanity to toiling ants in an unseen master's garden, and offers no refuge or remedy for the disease of amorphous chaos which is the true state of the universe. If his projection of fear and repulsion on people of color as agents of the Other was a prevalent feature and not a bug, he was hardly unsparing of the white Eurocentric culture which was his self-proclaimed birthright. Even in "The Rats In The Walls," which claims for HPL the kind of bucolic British aristocratic inheritance that he longed for in life, the foundations are revealed to be rot, abomination and insanity, and the principal antagonists of his key stories, while guilty of the supreme crime of miscegenation, are almost invariably white guys, with no savior of any color waiting in the wings.

Without getting dragged into a biography, it must be noted that Lovecraft's traumatic upbringing instilled in him an irrational terror of corruption and promiscuity that perhaps isn't so irrational, given that both his parents died in the madhouse of untreated syphilis. He went on to scrape out a bare existence as a ghostwriter and controversial but largely unloved pulp stalwart, but his body of work seethes with a nihilistic, misanthropic stew of which the racism is only the most acrid, superficial flavor.

So the art and the artist can't be separated without serious self-delusion. And it should be. He can't be rehabilitated by even the most sincere arguments of minimize his racism, which are as wishful and silly as revisionist fantasies that place him as the heroic gumshoe absent from his stories. And he shouldn't be. But with all due respect and sympathy to those who are done with HPL, I propose that, rather than relegate Lovecraft to the dustbin of dead white males, he should remain in the backwaters of literature but the forefront of outsider literature, of discordant voices whose false notes are as illuminating as their best.

That a self-taught and fiercely independent intellectual like Lovecraft could succumb so thoroughly to racist notions is an eloquent testimony to the virulent nature of racism as an intellectual pathology. It lends its cold, ugly comfort to the educated as well as the innocent by assuring the bigot they know everything they need to know about the Other, and need not feel strongly for them. The unwillingness of the modern Lovecraftian to confront the racism at the heart of his favorite stuff is an unwillingness to confront the racism and white privilege still baked into daily life almost a century after his death. It hurts to find out you've been wrong, and it can be devastating to find out that, hard as it's been, you've always been protected.

I learned more about the insidious corrosion of racism from reading Lovecraft than from any number of history books on the subject, and in writing my own contributions to the Cthulhu Mythos, I've been challenged to examine my own assumptions about everything that goes into my fiction, to consider as often as possible an audience as different as conceivable from myself, and to invite them inside. But I can't pass this off as more than a rationalization for my own quite unreasonable obsessions, and I wouldn't seek to wave away the misgivings of people who find his work insupportable. But it's worth examining why we even if we might not love Lovecraft anymore, we still need Cthulhu.

For one thing, it is worth considering the paradox of the radically inclusive cult of Cthulhu. While not much more diverse than any other subgenre of geek culture, the Lovecraftian community has no organized right wing like the sad puppies, no vocal alt-right or anti-feminist elements taking up the fallen standard of Lovecraft as a conservative icon, which is kind of weird. Radical conservatives already live in a fantasy, and they need somebody, anybody, more approachable than Hitler to snap off their stupid salutes to, and yet there seems to be little or no overlap between the Lovecraftians and the loudmouth assholes making a dog's breakfast of every SF authors gathering.

One reason for this is, we don't tolerate them. When Bob Price espoused nativist rhetoric in his lamentable keynote address at Necronomicon in Providence in 2015, he was roundly denounced by the convention's organizers, by a blazing majority of the programming participants and attendees, and by me at that weekend's Cthulhu Prayer Breakfast. He hasn't been invited to subsequent cons or to the Lovecraft Film Festival since, and reactionary Lovecraft defenders have largely ceded the field of debate and become entrenched in social media bunkers, while the rest of us continue to foster inclusivity and embrace the more progressive evolution of the New Weird.

Another reason is, Lovecraft isn't much of a red-blooded poster-boy for the kind of bellicose, alpha-male empowerment alt-right glibertarian geeks look for. Unlike Robert E. Howard—who has never faced the same scrutiny as Lovecraft but could easily be conflated into a redneck Mishima by muttonhead wingnut fans—HPL's mythos diminishes all human agency and sneers at their religious faith, indeed suggests that maybe the inscrutable Other, with his salacious rhythms and savage rituals, may be the one with all the answers. Solipsistic to the end, they need to remain at the center of a subservient universe, and the gibbering of passive academics unhinged merely by discovering the pseudopod-heavy secret face of nature is sort of a drag.

And why would any of this appeal to anyone, exactly? Lovecraft's pulp existentialism put faceless faces and vowel-challenged names to the creeping fear that the universe is alive teeming with intelligence, but none of it is for us. It captures and turns to lurid new purposes the emptiness of ennui, and puts a deliciously paranoid spin on contemplation of the centerless void that is our universe. In a world where no joke can keep up with the news, HPL's hysterical solemnity, his protestations of repulsion that go so far beyond too far as to become a kind of fetishistic hate-fucking of the unknown, are phenomenological implosions of rationalism so potent they somehow retain their capacity to inspire awe even after their histrionic, anachronistic style, disinterest in characters with agency or organic desires, and yes, parboiled racism, have been dealt with.

Modern cosmic horror writers and artists look to all that Lovecraft feared and reviled, that miscegenated, mutated polymorphous perversity that is the Other, and we say, "Yes, please." We embrace the Other not because it is awful, but because it is wondrous in its terrible beauty. We embrace and dissolve ourselves in the exotic and alien because the world is far stranger than any self-educated white New England Yankee's wildest fever-dreams, and we are a part of it. We embrace Otherness in all its forms, even in its most inimical and enigmatic face, when it looks at us in the mirror. The apocalypse we look forward to is not an end of old things, but an end to lies and the rise of beautifully weird new things, which shall not command but intrinsically earn, our devotion and worship.

Lovecraft himself said it best and proved himself a prophet after all, even when he was just trying to freak himself out.

At the closing of "The Shadow Over Innsmouth," the narrator finally devolves to acceptance when he learns that the awful taint of the alien abominations he narrowly escaped can never be purged, for it runs in his own blood.

It's not what Lovecraft represented as a model to be emulated, or as a trustworthy guide in realms of dream, that keeps his work and controversy alive. He never should have been the face of a literary prize, nor should any mortal artist (but the Karate Kid trophy still kinda sucks). It's precisely because his howls of atomized entitlement so vividly depict the violent dislocation of the rational western mind when confronted by the indifference of the cosmos, that he is so inexhaustibly inspiring to others who don't share his prejudices, indeed to many who categorically reject his characterization of most of humankind.

Though most of weird fiction has evolved past Lovecraftian pastiche and even explicit use of Mythos tropes, and rightfully so, discarding Lovecraft and relegating him to the margins would encourage Waffle-SS cosplayers to come out of the woodwork and claim him, and by extension the roots of cosmic horror itself as their own, and the Cthulhu Mythos would go the way of Pepe the Frog and tiki torches. If you're sick of Lovecraft now, wait until the alt-right claims Cthulhu as a meme. Once that happens, the party's over. The LA punk scene had to work tirelessly to call out Nazis and skinheads to stop them co-opting what they built, to keep a vital outsider scene from falling into the hands of elimationist imbeciles.

We may not unconditionally love Lovecraft, but we still need Cthulhu, damn it. (If you're offended, go home and make up a better mythology, then we'll need you, too.)

If Cthulhu did not already exist, it would be imperative to invent it, and over and over again, people have. The Flying Spaghetti Monster, absurdist parody of religious extremism, is only the latest shapeless cosmic sphinx to put a saucier face on the same set of tropes.

By a unique quirk of fate, Cthulhu is the great anti-brand, a cultural signifier ready-made for poking at human arrogance. Though he wore his influences on his sleeve, Lovecraft synthesized the deepest anxieties of the era into a coherent form and, whether by accident or design, gave it away to his fellow writers and the culture at large. While American fantasy icons like Edgar Rice Burroughs and Walt Disney fiercely commercialized

FORBIDDEN FUTURES

and policed their intellectual property, Lovecraft gave away the keys to his small but rich kingdom and so unwittingly created, in this age of total brand awareness, an open-source mythology as robust as any indigenous folklore, but as powerfully modern as any chain-smoking French philosophy.

This, as much as anything else, insures that the Mythos will never become tentpole Hollywood fodder, because no self-respecting hydra-headed corporation would put down hundreds of millions for intellectual property it can't exclusively own and exploit. In spite of hacky fanfic anthologies and plushy, cuddly overexploitation, Cthulhu continues to command a place in the hearts of people who love, rather than loathe, the strangeness of our universe.

While Lovecraft has rightly been pilloried for his failings as an artist and human being, he can't respond. He's dead. He shouldn't be held as an ideal, but as a progressive with more than a few appalling racists who should know better in my own family; I've had to learn how to navigate the straits between the lovable and loathsome territories in a single heart, to learn even from the worst.

While Lovecraft falls out of fashion largely due to political fatigue, Cthulhu recedes even now from the market because of overexposure, its mystery largely depleted by cheap and lazy pastiche and cut-and-paste hack-work. But as you cruise these pages and delve into the stories, you'll see how, in the hands of sorcerers such as the inestimable Mr. Dubisch and the amorphous cabal of literary magi assembled herein, the mystery itself is inexhaustible, waiting only for the proper signs, invocations and sacrifices, to be reawakened.

The tense extremes of horror are lessening, and I feel queerly drawn toward the unknown sea-deeps, instead of fearing them. I hear and do strange things in sleep, and awake with a kind of exaltation, instead of terror... stupendous and unheard-of splendors await me below, and I shall seek them soon. Ia r'lyeh! Cthulhufhtagn! I shall not shoot myself, I cannot be made to shoot myself!

We shall swim out to that brooding reef in the sea and dive down through black abysses to cyclopean and many-columned y'ha-nthlei, and in that lair of the deep ones, we shall dwell in wonder and glory forever.

-H. P. Lovecraft

GOODFELLOW'S GUIDE TO THE OLD ONES

CTHULHU

-Octopoid head, vaguely anthropomorphic body, may or may not have wings.
-Serious inferiority complex.
-Infects entire human race with nightmares stirring in his sleep, but can be mortally impaled on the prow of a fishing smack.
-Because idols of Great Old Ones tend towards allegorical rather than depictions, and his features may simply represent mastery of all that swims, flies or walks, may not look like this at all. We have only a sailor's account and a lot of plushies to go by...

HASTUR

-Hates being paged on intercoms.
-Surly that people he hates don't offer more sacrifices to him.
-Basically hates everything; why do you keep inviting him over?

CTHULHU SPAWN

-Your general features, but boneless pseudo-pod limbs, wriggling facial tentacles and the milkman's eyes.
-Cute now, but they grow up...
-You're paying for it to go to college; it'll probably flunk out and blame you.

OUTER GOD

-Misbegotten trust-fund spawn of unfathom-
able cosmic copulations.
-Could look like anything... even this book!
-Nowhere near as impressive as an Inner God,
but pretends never to have heard of them.
-Brags incessantly about eating planets you've
never been to.

SHUB-NIGGURATH

-Black Goat of the Woods with A Thousand
Young. Guess who's feeding them?
-Easily mistaken for a malevolent, sentient,
ambulatory, unspeakably fecund tree with a
Thousand Young.
-Claims to be really spiritual, but incessant-
ly tells gross cougar hookup stories.
-Horns don't always mean she's horny.

DEEP ONE

-Scaly green complexion, hopping gait,
MAGA hat.
-Less human every year, but angry that YOU
haven't been deported yet.
-Constantly bitches about Millenials ruining
things; can't log on to own wi-fi system.
-You think YOU'RE having a mid-life crisis?

NYARLATHOTEP

-999 forms and avatars, but always shows
up in the same dingy clothes.
-Abuses "brutal" and "hella" as adjectives.
-Accepts sacrifices, never delivers apocalypse.
-Gives you a ride to the hella brutal metal
show in an alternate dimension, leaves you there.

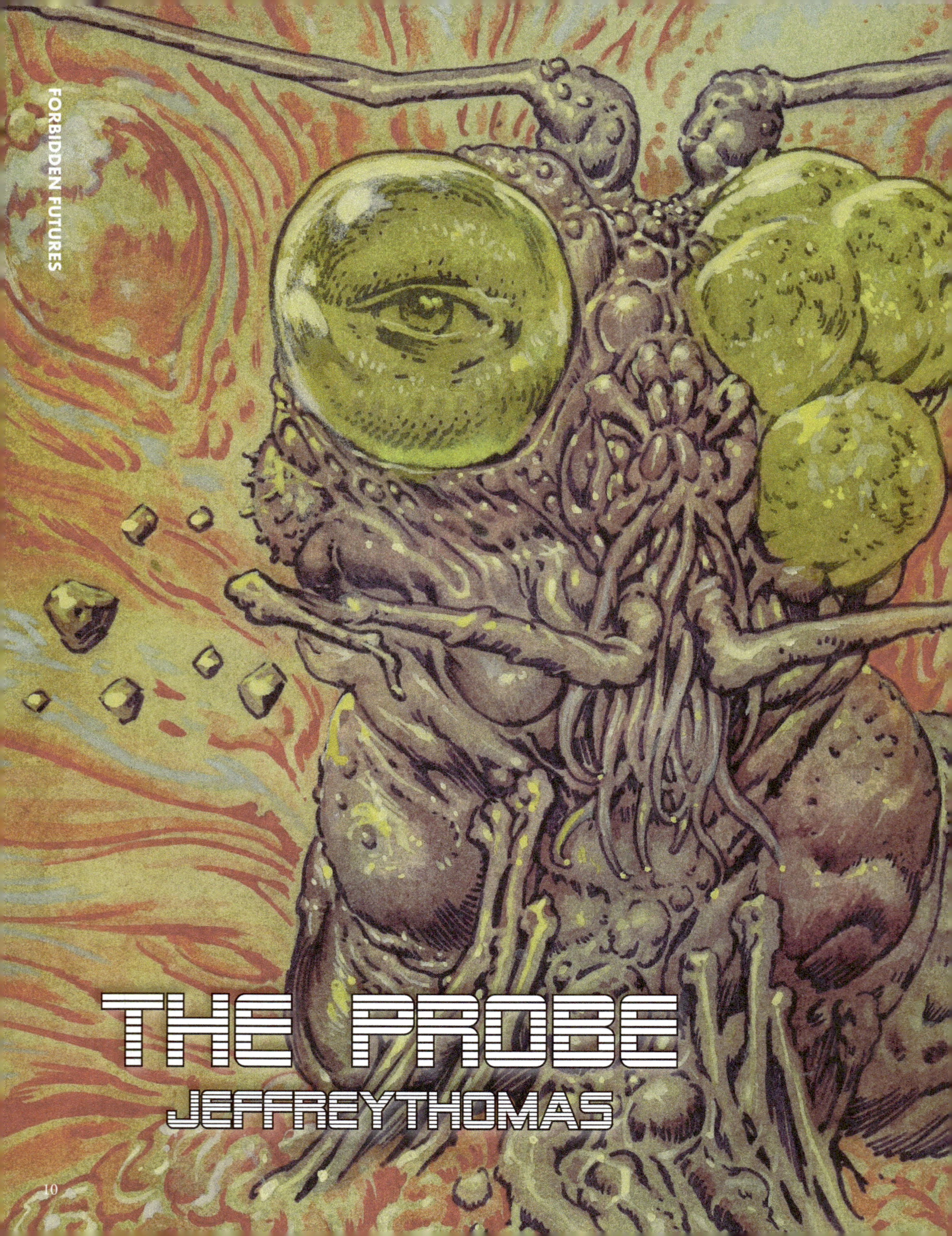

FORBIDDEN FUTURES
THE PROBE
JEFFREY THOMAS

OVER THE YEARS, researchers at the gosston observatory for extradimensional study had developed a variety of means of peering into alternate worlds that couldn't be crossed into bodily by their exploration teams. Great telescope-like instruments could gaze into some realms. Mechanical probes with cameras and sensors could be sent into certain worlds into which the passage of human beings, even in protective suits, was not possible.

Symmonds had been trying to find a means to pry open a peephole into Dimension 472 for months. He had discovered no method of looking into D-472. Still, there were other ways in which data could be gathered, and his most sensitive sensors had finally recorded electrical activity beyond the curtain between this world and D-472—voltage fluctuations consistent with the ionic currents of the neurons of human brains.

He had projected magnetic beams into D-472, trained them on the areas of such activity, managing to capture vague resonance images of the brains of a number of the unseen beings dwelling there.

Symmonds had brought his results to his higher ups, and obtained permission to take his researches further. Though it was not possible to send a human being into D-472, it was feasible to port over a much simpler life form. And fortunately, at GOES they had developed a number of types of bioengineered organic probes for this very purpose.

He ported over one of these tiny parasites, directly into the center of one of these loci of neural signals.

The minuscule creature—something between an insect and a slug—its own neural activity tied into his systems, would be his remote eyes. Ultimately perhaps even literally, if it could find its way to the ganglion cells that converted light rays into the electrical signals that gave this shadow being its sight. If it could patch into those cells, transmit to him what this inhabitant of D-472 saw through its eyes, then Symmonds would be like a demon that possessed it. (He might even have attempted to play long-distance puppeteer, influencing this being's actions and behavior, except that would be unethical. His intrusion must be a passive one; voyeur, not molester.)

His researches were put on hold, however, when not long after Symmonds ported over the organic probe he became afflicted with excruciating headaches. He had to take time off from work to rest, and when the headaches didn't abate—only intensified—he admitted himself to Gosston Hospital's ER. There, scans revealed the problem: an anomalous stowaway in his brain, that had been growing in size as it nibbled through his tissues on its way to his ganglion cells.

To his embarrassment, Symmonds realized his instruments had been rebounding signals off some interdimensional obstruction. There was no D-472; it was only a mirror reflection of this world. And, as the transmissions he recorded from his organic probe later confirmed—images of concerned ER personnel leaning over him, mouthing comfort to him—the brain he had ported the probe into was his own.

MASKS

BY ORRIN GREY

"You were his friend, right?"

His granddaughter's voice on the other end of the phone, her words clear and free of static. I wait to answer, don't want to, because how do I say, "I don't know?" For months now, he has been coming over to my house to play *xiangqi*

two or three nights a week while we drink hard cider and talk about bullshit. Does that make us friends, or just two lonely old guys with nobody else to talk to?

Whatever I feel in my heart, what comes out of my mouth is bound to be an affirmative, because what else can I say? And besides, she is so far away—London, of all places, with children of her own that I can hear in the background—while I am so close— his own townhouse just two doors down from mine, only empty spaces between us, because this neighborhood is dying, just as he was dying, just as we all are dying. One uncomfortable phone call at a time.

She hasn't said the words, but the implication is clear in her voice. If I don't do it, men will come. Strangers. Impersonal men who will throw it all into boxes and, from there, who knows? The Goodwill? The landfill? No place where it matters. No place where it will be appreciated.

Am I the old man's friend? I don't think so. Do I want to do it? No. So why do I say yes into the receiver, my voice bounced across thousands of miles to his granddaughter in London?

The answer is guilt. No more noble a motive than that. I think that I know what to expect, when I open the door. He came to my house so often, after all. I couldn't help but smell it on him. Dust, old food smells, stale cigarettes, the scent of clothes left too long in a closet. All the aromas of a college professor gone to pot.

That there are drifts of paper and take-out food containers keeping the door from opening all the way comes as no surprise, either. The old man was a hoarder. No shock there. Piles of things in every corner. A microwave, door hanging partway open. One blender, another. A DVD player still in its original box, the tape unbroken.

The layout of his house is identical to mine, and so stepping inside feels both familiar and strange; a post-apocalyptic movie in which well-known landmarks lie in ruins, or are half-consumed by plant life run riot.

Just as in my place, the living room is the largest one in the house, eating up much of the ground floor. Books lie piled on the carpet, along with cup noodles, coffee filters filled with old grounds, overflowing ash trays. There is almost no furniture in this room. Just an amber floor lamp and a purple recliner that looks to be made of lichen, as if I would sink into it forever were I to sit, sending up a cloud of recliner spores in my wake.

In the fireplace, where my TV sits, he has piled empty bottles, jars, old photographs, hand-written letters. A nonsense shrine, built by a man whose religion was his own and no one else's. In one bottle, a beetle crawls, too large to ever escape its prison.

My eyes skim it all but they settle, of course, on the masks. I knew, dimly, that the old man had once worked in Poverty Row Hollywood, but I had forgotten what job he did—makeup, set painting, and masks. He said once, *"Whenever a detective or a tortured academic stood in front of a wall of masks—masks from Bali, from Africa, from wherever the studio thought conjured the exotic—those might*

have been mine. I was cheaper than shipping something in. Easier than doing your own homework."

The masks on the living room wall aren't those, though. No studio in the 40s would have let even Patric Knowles or Ann Sheridan stand in front of these things. The faces, trapped somewhere between human and monster, between being faces at all and being something else: stars, galaxies, other organs.

Melting, running, racing from one to the other and back again, only to become lost somewhere in the middle.

In the dim light struggling in through faded, half-closed blinds they seem damp, alive. Many tongues twitching, many eyes darting. Where did these masks come from? How did the old man come by them? Do they predate the old movie masks, or did they inspire them? Did they come *from* the old man or did they come *to* him? Muse or creation?

These are the questions that assail me as I stand in the quiet of the house, dust motes surrounding me as I breathe in the smell of rotting food and spores and who know what else. When my house is quiet, I can hear the traffic on the highway, but in his living room I seem to hear something else. Scuffling. Breathing. Panting. Clawing.

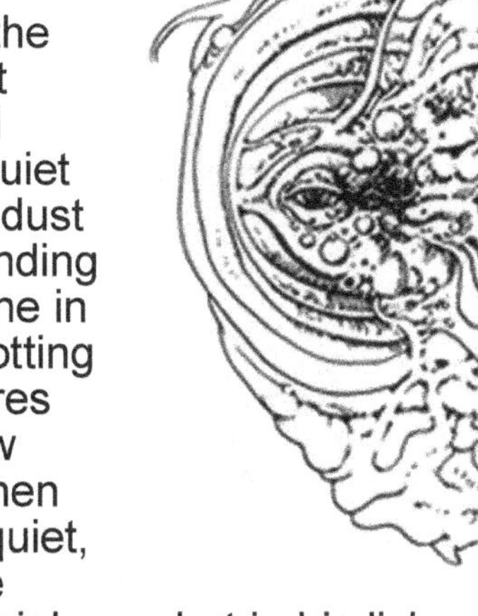

I walk nearer to the masks, and the sound rises. Do they see me, as I see them? They look agonized, starving, desperate. They remind me of the old man. I reach up my hand, let it hover in the air in front of the nearest mask, and I *know* that its features recede even as they also creep closer, though I could never prove it.

I feel the purple recliner against my thigh, and when I look down it seems so *inviting*. I could sink into it, I think, chair spores floating up and into my lungs. I could wait there, keeping the masks company until someone else comes to try to take them down. An hour, a minute, a second ago the idea would have appalled me, but now?

Now it sounds so fine…

SUJN'S LITTER

MATTHEW M. BARTLETT

SUJN SNAPPED AWAKE, AWARE AT FIRST ONLY OF A THROBBING PAIN AT HER MIDSECTION.

Then came a sensation of incremental loosening, as of having been relieved of a heretofore unperceived physical burden, its profundity noticeable only in its absence. The gravel on the flat rock on which she lay bit at her back, at her flank, at her heels. She popped open one eyelid, then the other, sending shards of sleep scattering. Through a haze of crusted lashes she saw that the sun had only just begun to brown the sky.

Then came wet, squelching sounds, as of skin peeling away from tacky plastic. Something chattered high and raspy, and then screeched. A second voice chimed in, and then a fair chorus. Sujn's hand went instinctively for the dagger she kept at her side. This sudden movement caused the agony to reassert itself below her belly; now pushing its way up through her chest to her upper arms, down to her thighs. Her head wrenched back, pulling a neck muscle, and salty tears poured into her ears.

Then the pain came in her legs, piercing, stabbing. She sat up, pulling her feet up against her buttocks, and there they were, newborns, six or eight of them, small, fierce-faced, wet with her blood, stabbing at her calves and knees with their nails. They were strong-muscled, hopping, hovering, trying out their nascent wings. They panted with exertion, little tongues jabbing downward, fine drips of bluish drool spotting the sand-covered rock.

One of them jammed a nail in between her patella and femur. Screaming, she drove the dagger up through both of its hearts and its neck into its brain. As the blade passed under its ribcage, its eyes widened, the hateful stare dulling and going blank. She struggled to her feet, and shook the child from her dagger. The others looked warily at her, and down at their fallen brother, who was diminishing as they watched, muscles deflating, skin rippling and fluttering.

Time slowed. The sun bobbed as it approached its apex, the sky the black-veined light brown of morning. Before very long it would deepen, darken, go again to charcoal. A wind kicked up, blowing sand around them. The little ones crouched, hate in their eyes. They lunged.

The rutting had been swift and fierce yet fumbling, devoid of rhythm, too much and somehow not enough, cut off with a grunt and a stumbling dismount. Her sated suitor swaggered off, the sand raising his skirts and his hair, and she hated him and his stupid jutting jaw and too-small eyes and yet she wanted him to

return. She despaired of her weakness.

A school of migrating ferkels rushed past. She snatched one up, and chewed into its neck more savagely than was necessary, inhaling its shrieks and letting its blood coat her throat. She knew she was eating too fast, that ferkels are rich, their fat-laden livers to be savored slowly. But the hunger was too much to bear. Later, she threw the whole up in a steaming pile. Retching piteously, she fumed, hungry again, but angry and feverish and foggy, and curled up to go to the dark and quiet place where everything fell away and was, for a hard-to-quantify section of time, peaceful.

She stepped on the foot of one, then stove in its forehead with the pommel of the dagger. She released its foot as it crumpled, a round dent in its forehead, and kicked her leg hard, detaching another from her calf, sending it rolling into a leaning cairn. The rocks toppled, burying it. Only the tips of its fingers were visible, trembling and twitching. A third jumped on her back. She dropped her sword and beat at it with her fists, feeling its hot breath on her fingers, until it finally fell and curled up, breathing hard. She reached for her fallen dagger, only to see it rise glinting in the air before her, in the hand of a fifth. He jabbed it at her throat, just penetrating the skin, and with her left hand she grabbed the child's arm and twisted, with her right pulling away the dagger.

The others scattered, whimpering and hissing and glaring back at her as they fled. It was done. A beat of silence. Another.

Then from behind the cairn came a chirp and a trill. The last one poked its head out, slowly approached, pausing to sniff at the fingers of his fallen brother. She pointed the dagger. The child ignored it. She froze. Something about this one. In a moment he stood before her, his nostrils fluttering, taking in all of her smells, pupils large and black. Curious. She jabbed the dagger into the earth and bent, lowering her hand to the ground, palm up. The child boarded. She lifted him to face her. He pushed his face forward and they shared a small kiss. Her head whirled. She felt a dizzying rush of inexplicable emotions. Then hunger growled in her belly, a ululating, insistent lamentation. She considered. The child saw it in her eyes. His pupils grew, filling his eyes like oil. He bared his teeth and hissed. She gasped. The sky went at once to pitch, obscuring the blood, but not the screaming.

"I like your eyes," her murky voice framed by the nearly closed bathroom door.

Beads of sweat dampened my forehead, "I'll be on the balcony." Her penthouse was beautiful, even if uncomfortably warm. I slid the glass door open and entered the relief of the nighttime air and the awe-inspiring view. Fifteen floors up is sweet. There were feathers here and there that avoided my footfalls as I strode to grasp the railing and then pressed forward to look past the ledge. A crisp gust and swirl of feathers bit me and I retreated inside. "You own a bird?" my voice elevated to rise above the soundscape of *"The Flight of The Valkyrie"* and also penetrated the bathroom door.

"Do you like classical music?" she had asked at the club. Of course it's yes to whatever a hottie asks when it comes to music. Except for country. But it was the kiss that followed after several drinks that brought me here. *"Let's go to my place and listen to some music."* Life is too good and too easy.

"What are you doing in there?"

"Getting ready," she cooed. "Is the playlist not moving you?"

"The music is great. I just, well, you know."

"Patience."

I took another tour, my eyes now accustomed to the dim lighting, and peeked into what appeared to be the bedroom. The bed was enormous. Like California king big or bigger. You could have a party on that monster. I opened the door further and stepped in and was greeted by a wave of nauseatingly humid heat. Taking a seat on the bed I promptly sank into the nest of comfort. I reclined to relish the down-filled mattress and realized that the ceiling was unbelievably high and there was a trapeze bar hanging above.

"Hey, where's your bird?" I propped myself up to look around the room. There was only a distressed wood dresser the length of the room with several large decanters arranged for decoration. They were filled with large marbles submerged in water.

"Are you in my bedroom?" she called from the bathroom.

"Yes."

"You said you were going to the balcony."

"Hope it's okay. I'm not trying to be forward but when you kissed me earlier I thought you were going to devour me, so I . . ." the large marbles seemed to be staring at me. I stood to take a closer look at the decanters.

"I said patience. I was removing my make-up," she was approaching the bedroom.

Teetering on unsteady legs, I wiped my sweaty brow; the heat and drinks were taking their toll. I leaned on the dresser and peered through the thick glass at the strange marbles. They peered back. I lurched backwards onto the bed.

"I really like your eyes," her silhouette framed by the door.

My vision had to be failing because she appeared to have bird's wings.

"I think I'll keep them."

HARPY
TED WASHINGTON
ISSUE TWO - OTHERWORLDLY

SLITHER EYES
JOHN SHIRLEY

CLORISSA HAD BEEN WADING ALONG FOR A LONG TIME. SHE WASN'T SURE HOW LONG, BUT HER LEGS WERE SHAKING FROM FATIGUE. HER CALVES WERE CRAMPING. THE EXTRA WEIGHT ON HER HEAD, SO LIGHT AND LOVELY BEFORE, NOW FELT HEAVIER.

But it still felt beautiful. The man with the tattoos on his face, blue and green images of soft clutching things, had said that the drug would take her into another world, and it had. It had gone down, then up, like a flower blossoming seen in fast action, all sped up, from the seed in her belly, sprouting, coming up in her throat—she had choked at first but the feelings were so beautiful she didn't care—and then it came up out of her mouth. She felt it sliding from her mouth up her face, toward her eyes, crawling damply, luxuriantly but forcefully up and up, and then the blossom—a thing of flesh as much as plant—poised over her eyes. It had split in two—then its two dart-shaped flowers had driven straight at her eyes. A double piercing pain, as it slithered into her eyes, as it burst them... Destroyed her eyes entirely.

She didn't mind. The pain was part of the glorious, every changing painting in her mind. The bursting of her eyes was part of the painting too. It was the most beautiful image she'd ever seen. Pain and pleasure were all intertwined in it. It pulsed with life and awareness. It looked at her as she looked at it. The pleasure the slithering plant was giving her was sexual and far beyond sexual; it was so profound, so all consuming, that the pain was like a tartness added to a sweet drink, a perfect counterbalancing. The pain was exquisitely integrated into the pleasure; into the beautiful living, transforming painting her mind had become...

She was a painter, was Clorissa, and now she thought, could I ever paint this, in my dank little studio, could I evoke a tenth of this alien glory?

No. Clarissa was the work of art now. She was living it, instead of painting it. She was sightless, in some ways—her eyes were gone; her eye sockets full of something else; her heart thudding in tandem with another heart, with the thing that had enveloped her entire head. Sightless she saw all, an infinity of gold and scarlet, liquid emerald and melting diamond, constantly shifting, yet always asserting patterns, slithering away from the center and returning...

Blind but all-seeing! Her nervous system charged with pleasure but crackling with agony. That's how she'd felt for hours, and even after she felt herself stripping off her clothes, walking blindly but with surety out the door into the swamp behind the house where the tattoo man had his special sessions. She had felt the warm, close air sliding over her skin; she felt the mud enveloping her feet, the water about her ankles, as she walked in the shallow water, slipping a little but somehow always recovering. Her body knew just where to go. She wasn't afraid of the gators. She sensed them gliding along the surface of the swamp water nearby. But she knew they wouldn't come close to her. She could even get glimpses of their small, reptilian thoughts. They saw the glorious Other wrapped around her head and they were afraid of it.

The Other spoke to something else, something bigger, something waiting up ahead.

The mud got deeper, creeping up to her calves; the water deeper now, up around her thighs, lapping at her hips. It was amazing she could walk along blindly and not fall, though her vision was transfixed by the glorious vision, the slithering mass of beauty, like thousands of baby snakes intertwining with infinity...

The other was guiding her. She heard its heart, and began to hear some of its thoughts.

"This one is almost exhausted. It was the only rapid way to reach you... He planted me deep within her...he serves us well..."

Now the colors swarming Clorissa's vision were dimming, going dark; the sinuous shapes taking on browns and grays, becoming sluggish in their movements. Pain began to overbalance pleasure. It spread out like cracks in an old, dried up painting. A painting of her, Clorissa, in some forgotten basement, covered in mildew, flaking away...

She felt a plunge in her heart, an engulfing darkness. She wanted to cry out, to beg for a return to the boiling infinite beauty, the painting engorging her mind, but she could make no sound. The other had enwrapped her head; filled her mouth as well as her eyes.

She staggered...and exhaustion took her, like a giant cold hand, and pressed her down to her knees. She was up to her breasts in water now, shaking...

"I see you. Come, and take me back to the Always Womb of our Underland, and take what remains of her as my gift to you..."

Clorissa was gagging, trying to vomit, as the thing withdrew from her—the thing that had given her oxygen and waves of pleasure and a beautiful image drawn from the deeps of her own mind. The thing that had guided her body and brought her here, someplace in the swamp...

Now it slithered from her mouth and eye sockets and away from her—leaving her in utter darkness. She could smell the swamp; could feel the warm muck, the glutinous water. She could hear the gators coughing. And she could scream now.

She let out a single long, long shriek that echoed between the cypresses that she could not see...

Perhaps, she thought, the gators will get me now.

But they were still afraid. They swam hastily away as another, the parent of the Other, arose and arched over her. Clorissa could smell it, an alien smell; she felt its otherworldly thoughts raining upon her...

Little remains of her. But. I. Shall. Feed.

WAXEN
CHRISTINE MORGAN

ANOTHER PACKAGE ON THE STOOP. The old bitch and her scented goddamn candles...the whole house smelled like a fruit truck, a florist's stand, a bakery, and a candy shop simultaneously exploded and then burnt down.

Sighing, he picked up the box. It got everywhere, that smell. Permeated everything. He kept his bedroom door shut but it still got in there. Into his clothes and hair. Coating his skin with waxy-feeling residue. People remarked on it. ut what was he supposed to do? The old bitch owned the place. The old bitch's disability checks paid the bills and then some. As long as they kept rolling in, he didn't have to get a real job. All he had to do was take care of things here.

Besides, the candles did help cover the sickroom stench.

He let himself in and yep, there it was, a faceful of citrus and spice, vanilla and roses, something that was supposed to be clean linens, something else that was supposed to be spring rain, a mingling melange of dozens more. Plus those whiffs of wax and smoke.

Clocks ticked, the ancient refrigerator hummed, and a stand-fan whirred as it stirred the musty-dusty perfumed waxy air. He went through to the kitchen and set the box on the counter. An idle glance at the label didn't tell him much.

C&C Candles, Lake Hali, The Hyades.

Never heard of them. She must've belonged to like six different candle-of-the-month clubs, not to mention guilt-gifts from distant relatives too busy to bother with actual visits.

He snagged a beer, popped the top, and took a long swig. A cheap brand, but he wasn't about to shell out for the good stuff when whatever he ate or drank ended up tasting like scented wax anyway.

Once he'd finished the beer, he held off on opening a second and decided to at least act as if he was doing his job. He picked up the box again—the logo on the label was creepy, though he couldn't quite pinpoint why—and carried it down the hall.

"Yo, Edith, you got another candle."

The sickroom scents grew stronger the closer he got to her room. Not urine; he kept her catheterized for that. Not shit either; the old bitch probably hadn't had a true bowel movement for years. Stale and sour sweat ... chemicals, medication, ointment ... the tang of alcohol wipes ... and ...

"Whew," he said, waving a hand in front of his nose.

And that, friends and neighbors, was *eau de cancer*, a body rotting from the inside out. Strong today. Very strong.

In her room, the air seemed thick with waxy particles. The wallpaper was more wax paper by now. Fussy antique sideboards or hutches or who-the-hell-knew stood around, covered with candles. Most were in little glass jars, white wicks rising, flames flickering above molten puddles.

"Edith? Still with us?"

The old bitch didn't respond. She was a mummified bundle of sticks and wrinkles, one eyelid sunken shut, the other half-lidded over a filmy, faded orb. Her mouth drooped slack. If not for the shallow hitches of her chest, he would've thought she'd gone and died on him.

How long and how well, he wondered, would the candles mask full-on decay? When she did die, nobody had to know, did they? The checks would keep coming until it was reported, and who else but him would be reporting it? Quitting the agency and claiming he'd been hired as her live-in was the smartest thing he'd ever done.

In the meantime, though, might as well go through the minimum motions.

"Let's see what this one is," he said when he'd dealt with the IV. He slit the tape—that logo, that weird symbol, what *was* that?—and opened the box.

Packing material ... plastic wrappings ... and aha, finally, the candle itself.

He hesitated, nose wrinkling. "Eugh."

Not in a jar. A squat, stout cylinder. Yellow, but not citrus-yellow, not lemon-meringue-pie yellow, not honeycomb yellow. A darker, nasty-somehow yellow. Earwax yellow. *Diseased* earwax yellow. Greasy. Greasy to the look and to the touch. Like poorly-rendered tallow.

And its scent ...

Not floral. Not fruity. Not candy-bakery-sweet.

Acrid sprang to mind. Alkaline. The bitter mineral salt flats by a strange lake. A warm lake. *Lake Hali? In the dry shadows of the Hyades where black stars shine sharp?*

No wick protruded from its top. It was just a cylindrical blob, greasy and unpleasant, and why was he holding it, turning it around and around? Leaving impressions of his fingers in its soft, luridly organic substance ...

Was it a candle?

It felt like butter. Bad butter. A bad, rancid lump of butter. Churned from the yellow milk of some...*thing* ...

He squeezed and met a gooey resistance, a squirming undulant sort of movement. He thought of insectile larvae in wet cocoons ... unborn malformed embryos slippery in congealed fluid ... boneless and gelatinous ...

As myriad inhuman eyes peeled open, as the first slick tentacles oozed to curl around his fingers, he heard a low and chuffing rattle-sound, and realized the old bitch was laughing.

FORBIDDEN
FUTURES

SYMBIOT
by Zak Jarvis

JAKE DIDN'T KNOW HOW HE GOT INTO THE INTERVIEW. HE DIDN'T REMEMBER WAKING UP, GETTING DRESSED OR ANY OF THE OTHER STEPS THAT WOULD'VE PUT HIM INTO THE ROOM.

The last thing he could remember was a disastrous first date. He didn't feel hungover, but Malcom's icy indifference clung to him worse than any binge.

Oh god, he rubbed his temples. How much did I spend on liquor last night?

Without this job he'd have to dip into the grocery money to make rent on his tiny, lonely apartment.

The view looked down on a city of glass gone coppery in the morning light, with no landmarks he could spot. Reaching down for his pockets, a nick in the table's veneer caught his shirt. Did he really have and wear dress shirts in this shade of purple? Papers at the other end of the table stirred as the HVAC kicked in.

The door whispered open with a stream of laconic office chatter from outside. Before he saw his interviewer he smelled the coffee.

Heaven.

A tall black woman sat opposite him. Her natural hair made a golden nimbus around her face in the morning light. Two shades darker purple than his shirt, her jacket weirdly reminded him of skin. With glossy white nails she tapped the table.

"Good morning," she said. "I'm Evangeline. What's your name? We don't need last names here."

He cocked his head.

"Jake," he said, trying to hold steady against a weird, rising panic.

"Jake this isn't what you think it is. We have a lot of ground to cover and its best to cover it quickly, so I'm going to jump right in. Drink your coffee, and if you have any questions, please interrupt to ask them."

"First of all, you don't remember how or why you got here. That's to be expected. We are—we're guests. Treasured guests! Of—of something more important and powerful than anything you've ever known. This office around us right now isn't exactly real," she said. "Table, please revert."

The dark of the veneer faded in blotchy clouds until the entire thing was a pale yellow-green. The table wrinkled. The wrinkles bulged and throbbed under his hands. No longer an office table, it felt like some kind of clammy reptile.

"This room is a mimic organism—an animal, taking this shape for our benefit."

Jake pushed his chair back and stood up.

This is a nightmare.

"Drink some of your coffee, Jake. I'm not lying to you and neither one of us is crazy. This is real. Are you ready to see a little more?"

He gingerly sat down and took the coffee. It didn't taste quite like any coffee he'd had. It was better. He felt the panic draining out of him, so fast he almost expected to see a puddle. It wasn't just a lack of panic, he felt centered and present.

"That's some kind of coffee."

"So let's get comfortable with that, first." She said.

Jake took a long drink of coffee and then ran his hands over the table-animal, really feeling it. The flesh bunched up and stretched beneath his fingers like a scrotum in a cold room. A strong brine scent had started to overpower the coffee smell.

"Where is this?"

"It's a place up alongside the world we came from. There are thinned out places. The Suzerain can reach through and bring us over."

"Okay. Show me the rest."

"We're still taking things slowly. There's too much for all at once."

Evangeline put her hand on Jake's.

"Chamber, you may revert. Keep the chairs."

The room contracted briefly then breathed out. At first, little happened. The color of the walls mottled, the floor softened slightly.

All at once the whole room sagged into a new shape, it took barely a second. Pendulous blebs extruded from the walls and began to glow blue, veils pulsed through the flesh of the walls and ceiling, the window went circular and the view outside changed. Carnelian light flooded the room.

As his eyes adjusted, Jake got a clear view of the outside.

In place of a sun there was a black hole in the sky that somehow also radiated bright, red light—red light that lit a landscape of jutting stone and vast skeletons. Batlike creatures crawled through the air leaving an oilslick trail behind them that eddied and dispersed. Not far below the window, processions of vaguely humanoid things trailed around matte black stones, their masses of tentacles glistening beneath the mercilessly unreal sky. The stones flashed crawling symbols that jumped from one to the next as the procession moved by them.

Jake finished his coffee, or whatever it was. "This is taking it slowly."

"I'm afraid so, yes," she said. "It looks— inhospitable—but the Inamoratrix have created a vast area for us to be comfortable."

"Suzerain? Inamoratrix?"

"We're not quite to that topic yet."

"How many of us are there here?"

"Sixty seven, I think. Well, Sixty eight now."

"How long will we be here?"

"As long as we'd like."

"What if we don't like?"

She laughed. "You'll see."

"Okay, what do we do here?"

"Read, watch entertainments, enjoy each other's company. Feast. All the usual things, really, just slightly different."

At least the chair is still a chair. "I get the impression there's something else."

"There is, but this is the hardest part to take."

She stood up and took off her jacket. Her blouse became diaphanous and veined as she started unbuttoning it. The two garments, dropped onto the table, curled up together and purred.

He thought she was going to take her bra off, but instead she turned her side to him. There was a bulging slit there, just below the ribs. As her fingers rode over it they dragged with them a sticky trail. Her breath hitched.

Jake felt something in him rise up to meet the moment. Like arousal, but also alien, worrying.

"Touch it," she said. "Don't be shy."

"I'm not—uh. I mean, women aren't my thing."

"There's no men or women involved here. Just touch it."

With an effort he reached out to touch the slit in her side. It parted open to meet his fingers and everted. His fingertips on her slick flesh made his body answer. The answer you might expect, but also from his own flank.

Jake's eyes went wide and he scrambled to lift his shirt. Before he could feel what was there, what was there felt his frantic hands and responded. His own hole opened to his fingers—wetting them, closing around them.

"What," he gasped. "What is this?"

"The Inamoratrix have modified us. This organism lets them—it lets them interface with us, and it feels very, very good."

THE HUMAN HABITATION AREA SEEMED TO GO ON FOR MILES. HE WANDERED THE PATHS OF A NATURE PRESERVE, TOURED SUITES, ATE IN A LARGE COMMUNAL DINING AREA, AND SAW ROOMS THAT COULD BE RECONFIGURED AT A WHIM.

Privacy was easy to come by, and Jake made use of it to test the new organ he'd been given.

As erotic as it was to touch the outside of it, putting his fingers inside felt wrong. The pressure inside it, the bulging on the walls— he could not forget those were his intestines being pushed around and it left him with a vague, sick feeling. All the same, he couldn't stop exploring the thing when he was alone.

But he wasn't alone for long.

Caleb caught his eye within five minutes of entering the human habitat. He was a bit shorter than Jake with wiry black hair and sharp blue eyes. They clicked immediately. A shared interest in French art house cinema and Italian exploitation got them talking.

"Deodato?"

"Oh Christ," Caleb laughed. "Don't get me started. Pure, filthy id. As transgressive as Passolini without the benefit of so much as a flinty chip of respectability. And as long as we're being honest, his films were really effective in helping me pass before I came out. So tragically het."

The next afternoon they fucked in Caleb's quarters.

He didn't touch Jake's slit until they'd exhausted the usual parts. Jake flinched away from Caleb's fingers.

"It doesn't make you feel uncomfortable?"

"You get used to it," Caleb said. "It just feels so good when they do it. Sorry for going there without your permission."

Jake laughed softly.

"As weird as this date is, it's *that* one I'm worried about. How much longer do you think I'll have to wait?"

Caleb took his hand.

"It should be pretty soon."

WHEN THE CALL CAME, JAKE FILLED WITH SUCH A BUZZY MIXTURE OF FEAR AND EXCITEMENT THAT HIS CLOTHES CHANGED COLOR CONTINUOUSLY. CALEB WALKED HIM TO THE EXIT FROM HUMAN HABITATION.

Inside the passage way the light of both suns cast opposing shadows across his path. The membrane of the passage became crystalline and Jake could see the black stone plain the building lived on. The outside ground appeared congealed, like a vast scab. His limited knowledge of geology offered him no help in deciphering the forces that had made the place.

The next passage segment filled with air from a sphincter in the ground while the one he'd passed through sealed and refilled with the viscous outside atmosphere.

Walking along with him, outside the hallway were tall bony creatures like bundles of sticks. Their beady eyes watched his every movement from beneath horned ridges on their elongated heads. The trail they left drifted and sank.

Jake's new organ pulsed in anticipation.

After some distance a last aperture opened and he was greeted by two roughly humanoid women. Bare chested and chartreuse green, they moved on powerful coiling tails. With bulbous eyes and fanged mouths they smiled at him.

He had to stop walking when his bowels threatened to evacuate, a sensation made more urgent by the pressure of the new organ.

They comforted him with their hands as though they knew why he'd stopped. When the cramping peristalsis passed he took a step forward.

Forward. To the liquid interface in front of what he could only call a throne room. A vast, seated figure observed him with huge hematite eyes. Its wrecking ball of a head trailed tentacles busily coiling and grasping at themselves. Behind it flexed massive wings.

The women were gentle. Urging him softly forward, they ushered him up to the interface between atmospheres. One of them spoke, a long, burbling sound like a clogged drain.

"Welcome, Jake!"

The words were clear in his head even if his ears heard something else.

"Today it is our honor to introduce you to your Inamoratrix. They will see to all your needs, you will want for nothing."

They both gently pushed him forward once more.

A figure on the other side of the interface detached itself from the giant Suzerain and slithered through the thick natural atmosphere. It was a creature similar to the ones who had escorted him, but taller, its face less human even if its breasts were startlingly so.

Their hands penetrated the interface and took Jake's. Warm and dry, the Inamoratrix's grip was strong as a rock-climber's. With a push they came entirely through. Eyes with multiple irises turned to meet him, moving in a strange nystagmus.

"Are you prepared, Jake? I will take you to a private chamber if you are," they said. "But we can wait until you are ready."

He gulped, only then noticing that his legs were shaking. "As ready as I'll ever be."

His new organ undulated. Its joy was his joy, but the terror was his alone.

The Inamoratrix took him through a series of hallways and chambers until they came to a place with a steaming, shallow pool and dim yellow light.

"Would you like to undress yourself, or would you prefer that I do it?"

Trembling, Jake took off his clothes, each piece falling to the floor only to crawl into a nearby alcove and fold itself neatly away. The Inamoratrix smiled at him and took his hands once more, leading him into the warm, viscous pool.

His terror began to dissipate a little, the way it does once you've begun doing the thing you're afraid of and there's no turning back. As he relaxed, the shape of the pool conformed to make him more comfortable.

"We do not have names or individuality the way you are accustomed, but if it would help you, you may name me." Their body next to his in the thick bath relaxed him even further.

"This is going to be a sexual encounter, isn't it?"

"Most would say yes."

"Would it bother you if I called you Robert, then? I've had good luck with Roberts."

"I shall be Robert for you," the Inamoratrix said, placing their hands firmly on Jake's chest. "Are you ready to let me inside you?"

He nodded, even though he wasn't sure at all.

The mouth in his side radiated ecstasy. He could feel it gaping, gulping up the fluid of the bath and expelling it.

Robert opened their mouth. Inside, hook teeth folded back, their red tongue bulged and flowered petals that rimmed the aperture until their mouth became something more like an anus, gaping open. Their throat bulged.

A glistening black beak emerged on a transparent, purple stalk.

They bent down, slowly, carefully, guiding the rounded beak to the opening in Jake's side. It nosed in the tiniest bit.

The intense pleasure was almost un- bearable, and while it was centered on the new organ, he felt himself starting to ejaculate.

Robert pressed their beak inside him.

Between waves of pleasure too intense to classify, Jake saw a small white pod slide down through the translucent stalk. The opening of the beak inside made him come again.

He'd never experienced multiple orgasms. It was like a natural force, a storm, crashing over him, swelling, then crashing again. Everything he was or had been crushed into a perfect, glittering diamond.

He couldn't even see.

The world came back to him in pieces: the sharp smell of his own body, his ragged breath, the organ's undulating grip on Robert's beak, the heat of the fluid on his newly-sensitive cock.

As the light faded back in, Robert spoke to him, apparently without the need of a mouth.

"I am ready to remove the interface. May I?"

The feeling of removal was one he knew, that emptiness of a lover withdrawn.

"You need to drink from me to ensure the viability of our young," they said, offering a breast.

He let himself be pulled down. Their breast pressed to his face, their nipple in his mouth. He sucked.

At first there was nothing but the warm, firm skin in his mouth. Then he tasted it, a drop at a time, metallic and watery, sweet, a flavor that seemed to change in waves until it was filling his mouth. It dripped down his chin. The organ on his flank squeezed. He felt it oozing under his clothes.

Torpor crashed down. It was a fight to keep his eyes open and he lost.

Robert fed him this way for days.

AFTER ROBERT LEFT, THE FEELING OF THE EGG INSIDE HIM WAS A PLEASANT REMINDER.

Why haven't I been this happy before? Is this some sort of mind control?

If it was, he was okay with it.

Once he'd run a marathon with coworkers who lived for running. It'd left him pleasantly sore for days. The aftermath of what he'd done with Robert was similar, a kind of windblown clarity from having been reduced to something so physical, so small and pure. All the nattering commentary and useless mental blather quieted for a while, as though in awe of what his body had accomplished.

When he returned to the human habitation area he could see in their faces that he'd changed, that he was truly one of them now. They laughed and ate together.

He and Caleb picked up where they'd left off and managed to enjoy each other's company outside the bed as well.

After a month Robert called him back to their quarters.

"I wanted to be with you at the end of the gestation," they said.

"What's going to happen? Will it hurt?"

"It won't hurt at all. The capsule I placed in you will pass through you back into your world. There is a feeling, but it is not pain."

Robert came closer to him.

"May I touch you?" they asked.

He nodded.

He felt the egg—the capsule—shift inside him, almost like gas. Robert gently put their hand on Jake's side, softly rubbing the contours of the slit through his clothes. The pleasure was less urgent, less ache than warmth.

There was a sensation like popping your knee after sitting for a long time—sharp, relieving—a cathartic pain.

"Congratulations," Robert said. "We're parents. You, us, and our Lord."

IT ALWAYS UNSETTLED JAKE JUST A LITTLE TO ACT AS FIRST INTERFACE TO NEW RECRUITS.

They stirred up the absence of his thoughts about the old life. He could remember it well enough, could vividly remember his struggles, but it nagged at him how little he cared about what he'd left behind. Like not bothering to pick up a dime he'd dropped.

Were all those people I left behind so worthless? The thought came more as a detached observation than an accusation.

After walking the freshly arrived Jessica through the introduction, he'd returned to his quarters with Caleb. They put on a late Cocteau film and turned out the lights.

It got easier and easier to live in the new world. He would not learn for quite some time the price they all paid.

WIDDERSHINS
Edward M. Erdelac

ON THE LAST NIGHT of the fairy Widdershins' watch over the girl Lakeisha Simmons, her uncle James staggered into her dark bedroom, stinking of the grave from which he had pulled himself. Within the festering heart of Lakeisha's uncle, curling like a thing unborn, Widdershins spied his old enemy, the incubus, Corngrinder. Corngrinder had been a saboteur in the Great Rebellion against Heaven, infiltrating human souls and tempting the lustful Grigori to the side of Lucifer.

Widdershins had engaged the incubi in the benighted huts east of Eden. That was how he had come to find himself abandoned when the cannons of Hell ceased and the Great Accords were signed. Many war-weary angels, loyal or otherwise, had deserted and been caught between when the borders of Heaven and Hell were sealed. These became the thoughtless fairies of man's legends, driven mad by their separation from the Creator. They established their lawless confederacy of dreams, Fluratrone, and forgot all past glories and iniquities.

But some, like Widdershins, dissatisfied with an eternity of purposelessness, sought a way in from the cold.

The Archangel Michael heard the solicitations of the good fairies, and gave them a path back into Heaven; guard the innocence of mortal children from the spawn of Lilith that assail in the night.

Lucifer likewise tasked his orphaned agents with the corruption of human souls.

Although the Rebellion was over, a Cold War of dreams and nightmares continued in the gray meridian between sleep and awakening.

Sometimes it spilled into the real world.

In two-hundred thousand years Widdershins had defeated countless bogeymen, goblins, and bug-a-bears, all intent on stealing the innocence of children. Widdershins had dragged them shrieking across the icy River Purgatory between Earth and Fluratrone, and sunk them in its frozen depths.

Lakeisha Simmons was to be his last posting, and this was the last night of her childhood.

Widdershins knew Uncle James mostly by his reputation. From his place in the walls he had seen Lakeisha's mother retreat in fright when her brother appeared at family functions, seen him eyeing the children strangely as they played. Lakeisha's father had driven James from the house, and Widdershins had heard whispers of drugs, abominable deeds, and prison time, and finally, with relief, of James' suicide.

Widdershins should have recognized Corngrinder's influence. The incubus had been grooming James, possibly perverting his whole miserable life, in preparation for this final, ghastly assault.

This battle would not be fought in dreams.

Corngrinder had poisoned James' heart until, at the moment of death, it became a cockpit for the incubus itself. Corngrinder had slipped in and assumed command of the physical vessel. Now, it piloted James haltingly across the room. As he bumped against the foot of the bed and fumbled with his belt, Corngrinder's intent was clear. What four thousand three hundred eighty spirits had been unable to accomplish with nightmares, Corngrinder meant to do by brute force.

But Widdershins had prepared. He flew to the back of Lakeisha's closet and dove into the dusty old teddy bear the family dog had eviscerated long ago. In his ungainly plush armor, Widdershins clambered over the shoeboxes and burst from the closet, pumping his stubby limbs, sprinting for the bed.

Corngrinder, through James, reached out jerkily for the sleeping girl. Widdershins sprang and pulled himself furiously up the coverlet.

Corngrinder pinched the pink drawstring of Lakeisha's nightie between James' dirty fingernails. Widdershins leapt from Lakeisha's pillow and grappled James' hand.

Instinctively, Corngrinder withdrew, bringing James' hand closer to see what had impeded it. Widdershins struck.

Beside the teddy bearskin, Widdershins had stowed a silver pendant. It had been a gift from Lakeisha's mother, lost under the bed years ago with earring backs and wayward toys. The purple box it had come in had been marked 'Paisley Park.' It was a glyph unknown to Widdershins, sharp angles curling around a plunging arrow, perfectly suited to the task at hand.

Widdershins swung it two-handed. Because it was a silver gift of pure love, it cut into the dead man's heart like an ax of lightning through a withered tree, impaling the surprised incubus nestled within. Widdershins rode the falling body to the floor, where, deprived of Corngrinder's animation, it splashed into puddles of inky shadow that coursed to the corners of the room to await the purge of dawn-fire.

Widdershins held his prisoner aloft, twitching on the arrowhead of the pendant, a sickly, blinking will-'o-the-wisp dripping red and firefly-yellow blood.

At the back of the closet, Widdershins hung Corngrinder from the hawser of his tug, an old discarded bath toy he had installed with a bodach's heart so that it could navigate the frozen Purgatory. The slow-burning heart had twisted the once smiling toy's face into a withering grimace. Corngrinder bobbed like an angler's ghostly lure, lighting the dark ice cracking before the scowling bow, and finally dwindled in the depths of the cold dark.

A greater light awaited Widdershins.

WE'LL KNOW THE REASON WHEN THE WORLD PARTS ITS LIPS BY JESSICA MCHUGH

THE MORNING THEY MEET, SHE FAINTS AT WORK AND CRACKS HER HEAD ON A DESK.

She begs him to go away, but he holds her hand and kisses her cheek, and as EMTs roll her past wide-eyed students, he whispers into all of her wounds. "No, my love. I'll never leave you again."

Screaming, she tries to leap off the gurney.

He looks human at first—handsome like Daddy—but just like Daddy, the beauty disappears in sinkholes that leave him a mangled, bulging version of himself.

Her body is the only one that matters, however. He knew and loved it ages before his perilous swim across the slick and clenching cosmos. It's the only reason he came. He tells her so and climbs on top, and writhing under his spongy, bloodless weight, she howls at the heavens. But the heavens have no ears.

The plates of her skull are loose and clacking as she rolls her head across the pillow, away from the green and white streaks of first and second and fifteenth opinions. When the medicine kicks in, reality and dream shrink and squeeze her mind like an octopus twisting its way through a colony of coral.

The inhuman creature at her bedside opens his arms, tentacles patched with thirsty cartilage emerge from his spongy flesh. They pretzel her body and fill every cell with I love yous that unfold like the stiff petals of a paper fortune teller.

She vomits down the front of her scratchy gown. Drenched and studded with blue and purple capsules, she thrashes, wriggles an arm free, and her fingernail snags a sagging blue-gray wrinkle under his left eye.

"But I came all this way," he whimpers, and his face rips like wet toilet paper. Watery brown meat spills from his exposed sinus cavity and gushes into her like the lukewarm freezer pops she dumped down her throat as a kid. Her pores open wide as the cosmic slit from whence he came, and his slushy guts fill her head with all the dreams he had of her in the womb.

He slept in lumpy, porous soil, waiting his turn to love something into metamorphosis. From the dawn of time, as microscopic slits blossomed around him in his quiet but teeming planet, his body grew slow. But love deepened quick, and with love came purpose, taking shape in him through the millennia, just as it ossifies in her now.

"It's not right," she cries. "I was good. I helped people; children."

"I'm a child," he says. "I've been so desperately lonely waiting for you. Help me. You're the only one who can. If you're as good as you say, you'll let me grow."

A version of her swallows more capsules and tries to kill his voice, but it feels like he's been there forever now. In her memories, he screams at her through achy knees and bad flus while, across the universe, planet built of him the perfect mechanism to devour the best parts of her.

If there were any. The longer he dwells in her, the more she doubts it.

He had doubts too, but they filled him with fire through the years. He forced every ugly thought to mutate from splendid mess to divine creation.

"I'll do the same for you," he says. "It's what we were born for."

An arrangement made ages ago, he explains, the greatest fortune she can hope to experience is being undone by an infinitesimal angel like him. There's no greater devotion than the love that reforms a stranger at the cellular level.

She asks him what will happen when her body can no longer house them both, but he has no answer, nor comfort except the knowledge that, although he will melt her bones and yellow her eyes and make of her a sloppy, screaming gash until the end, she is already one of many chasms opening in a New Mother Earth.

Upon surrender, she knows both of their histories but only one future. Tangled up in his tentacles, she will blossom like the galactic gashes come before, and within the planet speckled in suffering, his voice will diminish and eventually vanish.

It will be her turn to wait then. Centuries, millennia; maybe longer than him. But the day will come. Under the hood of a bloodless planet, she will leak her fever across the galaxy, and angels of death will fly from her lips.

POLYBIUS

READY PLAYER ONE By SCOTT R JONES

RIGHT, WELL, NOW THAT I'VE GOT YOU HERE, I CAN TELL YOU ABOUT POLYBIUS. THAT'S HOW IT ALL STARTED FOR ME. See, what the conspiracy theorists and urban legend chroniclers forget to tell you is that those Portland kids are still missing. Though by now, wherever they are, they're no longer kids. Once you fall into their hands you're basically clay. I could have been one of them, I had the high scores. A contender. I could've been clay.

Nearly a hundred thousand people go missing in this country each year. Imagine! You walk out the door one morning, and you never walk back in. Gone. Folks want to blame serial killers, cults, or the shadow government, but it's simpler, and uglier, than any of those. There are doors, see, and then there are doors. This continent is old, and it's rotten all the way down, full of holes, and some of those holes—they're doors. POLYBIUS was just such a door, only open for a few months, which is to say it didn't exist for long. I mean, try finding a console now. They may be ancient the way the dark between the stars is ancient, but that doesn't mean they don't like to try new things, when the opportunity presents. Who doesn't like to jiggle the handle of a new door, just to see what might happen if it opens? When it opens.

What did the old Ay-rab say? Their habitation is even one with your guarded threshold. Yeah, no shit, Abdul. Tell us something fresh.

The stories get one thing right. POLYBIUS was highly addictive. I remember the line-ups for the game, outside the Avalon and around the block, the fights that broke out when quarters lined up on the screen weren't honored, the faces that stumbled away into the night when the arcade closed. Those faces reflected something, and it wasn't light, but it felt so right.

POLYBIUS played you, you understand? Games back in the day required skill, sure, but they were essentially empty things, a shell to fill with your imagination and hand-eye coordination. But POLYBIUS wasn't there for you. You were there for POLYBIUS. That was the feeling, and it was electric. Stepping up to the console was like approaching an altar. As if you were tapping into something real, and vast, something majestic, and it only cost a quarter. A quarter! Nothing else like it. Reaching into the game through the joystick, the screen, you could feel them there. The interface went both ways. They would quest and probe, searching through you, for whatever it was you had they could use. I remember how it felt, that digital intimacy, that deeper than deep focus that burned the world away until it was just you, and the game, and whatever was on the other side of the game, connecting. I still dream about that connection, but it's never the same. I remember how it felt, and I remember when it went sour.

Did you ever see that Last Starfighter movie? Right? Kid beats a game and it turns out to be a recruitment strategy for an alien armada? Imagine doing that, and when they show up to take you off world to a life of cosmic battle and ripe space babes, the recruiter sniffs the air around you with a forked tongue and decides, well, maybe not. It seems mistakes were made, it hisses. That was me, son. I knew I was a good POLYBIUS player, great even, my high score went up early on and it stayed there, goddamnit. POLYBIUS did select me, I swear. It wanted me, or the things that seethed and breathed behind it did, and there's no feeling like that desire, when you're the subject. The door opened, and I should have gone through. But when it came my turn, they said no.

Since then I've done everything I can to find them, claim my right to wonder and glory. I've learned about the other doors, which at the end of the day are all the same door, really. Before it was POLYBIUS, it was a sealed box of black lacquered wood belonging to a bruja in Juarez. A fly-specked folio of living daguerreotypes in a Spitalfields shop. A mummified tiger penis enshrined in a Himalayan cave. Other, less comprehensible things, going back centuries. The Arab knew, and Chambers, and the Marquis de Sade. Hell, even Borges wrote about it, in that one story.

I've learned that those kids? Those kids had the right stuff, and POLYBIUS took them for a quarter. For me, well, the price is steeper. Sacrificial. I have to give them what they want, for as long as they want it, and then they'll let me through, I know it. No, you're not my first. This isn't some token thing they require. Takes dedication, skill. Think of it as a game, if that helps. And try not to struggle.

I don't need you throwing off my hand-eye coordination.

AS A PSYCHIC MIGRANT I'VE CAST MY SOUL INTO THE BODIES OF MAYAN AHKINOOB SCHOLARS, ROAMED INSIDE THE MINDS OF KOREAN HWARANG WARRIORS, PASSED FROM ONE KHOOMII SINGER TO ANOTHER ON THEIR VOICES. I'VE LISTENED TO THE SONGS OF ANGELS BUZZING WITHIN THE PARIETAL LOBES OF NEPHILIM. SWAM THROUGH THE AMNIOTIC SACS OF GESTATING SERAPHIM.

But on this psychic trip my peyote-addled brain cast my soul to a mysterious place. The beings populating this realm are unlike any entity I've dreamt of before.

A grotesque mockery of Octopoda and Teuthida, but land bound, drifting across the planet's surface with the aid of hydrogen producing organelles. Mucous rich pseudopods extend from their tentacles in profusion—whip-like fingers I imagine are capable of manipulating the environment with far more dexterity than human fingers. I sense these things are capable of building awe inspiring technologies beyond my comprehension, for their bodies are massive nervous systems; essentially brains with locomotion capabilities.

In my vision this species doesn't utilize any machines of violence; they wreak havoc across a populace with their very bodies. They raze inhabited cities, secreting organically produced nitric acids to dissolve any in their path.

There's a brutality here; capable of a kinder slaughter, they choose to inflict genocide with a cruel nonchalance instead. They're children who could put an insect out of its misery, but instead choose to pin its squirming body to a cork board. They delight in extinction.

Is this what is to ultimately be humanity's fate? We share our roots with a common ancestor, simple savage creatures, long extinct, roamed ancient Africa across sun scorched lands, may lay claim to our ignoble origins, before pen was set to paper, poems to music, brush to canvas. Will we alter our very genome so radically we no longer bear any resemblance to our primate lineage but become mollusc-like animals?

Perhaps our species had a less auspicious genesis, one on a landscape less veldt and more defined by vast deep oceans. Were we spawned beneath roiling surfaces whose depths remain unexplored? Or am I witnessing what has occurred far away, within the darker pockets of existence where no human mind has plumbed its depths?

As the End of Days nears neither scenario matters much.

Whatever dimension these things reside I know they're well aware of my psychic intrusion. They are not blind to my trespassing into their realm, and intend to trace my psychic-tether to Earth. They do not take well to being observed from afar. They take great offense at their existence being revealed.

They will visit quite soon.

Planets will split as they hunt me down. Galaxies that impede their progress will dissipate. They'll lay waste to any civilization ignorant enough to inconvenience their journey. Any and all obstacles will be removed to reach our universe.

There is so much more to tell, but even now I can sense those creature's passage, feel stars tremble into extinction as they pass. All things become extinct eventually.

Soon enough.

THEY DELIGHT IN EXTINCTION
CHRISTOPHER SLATSKY

KING C
BY NATHAN CARSON

I guess I've known about C since I was real young. Plush toys. Cartoons on the boob tube. Those ski masks with the yarn tentacles that say, *"I gave up on sex with other people years ago."* But it would be a lie to say I had an ounce of faith before I met Dolphin.

She used to come hear me sing at casinos on the strip. She said I did Glenn and Mr. Mojo Rising better than anyone. And Dolphin did *me* better than *everyone*. I couldn't help falling in love. She was always on my mind. I was hooked on her and she was high on Mythos. Pretty soon I started to see the lights in the water, which was a good trick since we lived in Vegas.

Pappy told me about that magician that made the Statue of Liberty disappear. How he sat in front of the screen and watched it go poof with a steaming Swanson dinner in his lap.

Dolphin and thousands like her had a pledge drive going to raise the big C right out of his slumber, into the homes of reality streamers everywhere. The crowd funding popped off because half the donors believed in him, and the other half—the ones with Miskatonic U bumper stickers on their Priuses— thought it was funny. They wouldn't have been laughing if they knew what was coming.

Dolphin moved into my penthouse. I was wrapped around her finger. We knew this event was our big shot at those fifteen minutes that only come once in a lifetime. Or is it four times an hour? I forget. The problem was that everyone wanted that spotlight to shine on *them*. We needed an edge.

Dolphin showed me the ads. Cosmetic surgery was no big thing on the strip. But a faceful of tentacles? Dolphin said I'd give the best mustache rides in Nevada, and I aimed to prove her right. In fact, I have, quite a few times. Just not with her.

We shared a taxi to the clinic. held hands and kissed, ready to take our love and faith to the next level.

We walked down the aisle to separate operating tables. "It's now or never," she said.

I went under the knife with a burning love in my heart. But Dolphin was a hard-headed woman.

When they unwrapped my face, she was standing beside me, pretty as can be. Only she still looked like her. And I looked like a seafood platter. I guess Dolphin got cold feet. When she saw me, she got all shook up. "Don't be cruel," I begged her. But she was just another devil in disguise. By the time the staples came out of my face, she'd already packed up her things from our heartbreak hotel and hopped an Amtrak for California.

That didn't pan out well, since the Del Yuge put the golden state underwater. When the cameras rolled and the chants were phrased, C didn't show up for his call. Well, a lot of us like to think that maybe he turned over in his sleep. One helluva bloop echoed out of Point Nemo, returning to sender. Sea level rose like an overnight sensation.

Maybe a couple hundred of us had the surgery, and made the cut—hand-selected by producers who practically drooled over our extreme makeovers. After the show was over, the sun still shined, the world kept turning. If you think getting a job is hard for someone with facial tattoos, well let me tell you what a bitch this was.

Lucky for me, only a couple dozen of the faithful had musical talent. And we all know that Mythos Rock is always a pretty limp imitation of the real thing. The only guys that really made a go of it stuck to death metal. That gave me a monopoly of sorts on the blue-haired buffet crowd.

My agent helped me distill the mash-up. The music of The King and the majesty of C. It was too dumb not to work. Just when tickets on the Carnival Cruise Subs started selling out, Disney California opened up like some bonafide trip to Atlantis. Well, let's just say I haven't collected a fun employment check for a few years.

Sometimes when I'm singing *"Suspicious Minds"* I'll look out the bay windows thinking maybe I'll catch a glimpse of her body drifting in that seaweed that sways all dreamlike in the fronds of palm trees lining the ocean floor. The rusting graveyard car lots, and the sunken stadiums remind me that the end is nearer than we think.

Here's the thing. C's been stuck on the porcelain throne of R'Lyeh pushing out a peanut butter and banana sandwich the size of Memphis for eons now. All things must pass, but some things pass slower than others. No disrespect intended, of course. I personally worked my way through *The Wheel of Time* on the shitter, so I have some concept of Cosmic Magnitudes.

Maybe C's gonna sleep for ten thousand years. Or maybe the big hunk o' love's planning his oft-prophesied 2068 Comeback.

All I know is that somewhere in that Pacific apocalypse is my Dolphin, singing the unchained melody that I hear on the crashing waves in my squid-faced jailhouse rock and roll dreams.

Uh, thankyouverymuch.

WAXEN

CHRISTINE MORGAN is an active force in the Portland bizarro and weird fiction scene. She's a regular contributor to THE HORROR FICTION REVIEW. She has also edited four books into the FOSSIL LAKE anthology series. Her other interests include cheesy disaster movies, modifying Barbie dolls, and working toward becoming a crazy cat lady.

THE PROBE

JEFFREY THOMAS is the author of such horror and science fiction novels as DEADSTOCK (finalist for the John W. Campbell Award), BLUE WAR, MONSTROCITY (finalist for the Bram Stoker Award), LETTERS FROM HADES, THE FALL OF HADES, SUBJECT 11, BONELAND and A NIGHTMARE ON ELM STREET: THE DREAM DEALERS. His short story collections include PUNKTOWN, GHOSTS OF PUNKTOWN, NOCTURNAL EMISSIONS, WORSHIP THE NIGHT, UNHOLY DIMENSIONS, THIRTEEN SPECIMENS, and THE ENDLESS FALL. Stories by Thomas have been reprinted in THE YEAR'S BEST FANTASY AND HORROR, THE YEAR'S BEST HORROR STORIES, and YEAR'S BEST WEIRD FICTION. Though he considers Vietnam his second home, he resides in Massachusetts.

HARPY

TED WASHINGTON is an artist, author and publisher based in San Diego, CA. He is the host of Palabra, a reading series held at La Bodega Gallery twice a month.

KING C

NATHAN CARSON is a writer, musician, and Moth StorySlam Champion from Portland, Oregon. His nonfiction can be found in the pages of WILLAMETTE WEEK, THE OREGONIAN, RUE MORGUE, NIGHTMARE MAGAZINE, DECIBEL, and countless other outlets. His fiction has been published in a constant stream of weird horror anthologies and magazines. STARR CREEK is his first standalone book. His recent graphic novel adaptation of Algernon Blackwood's THE WILLOWS is on comic stands now. Oh yeah, he is also a founding member of Portland's first doom metal band, WITCH MOUNTAIN, now celebrating its 20th anniversary. More info at *www.nathancarson.rocks*

SLITHER EYES

JOHN SHIRLEY is the author of numerous novels, including DEMONS and BLEAK HISTORY, and many story collections. He has also scripted movies, television, and comic books. His movies include THE CROW. He won the Bram Stoker Award for his story collection BLACK BUTTERFLIES: A FLOCK ON THE DARK SIDE.

SYMBIOT

ZAK JARVIS has lived in America's worst weather and its best before settling on permanent fog. His fiction can be found in numerous publications including the Stoker Award winning DEMONS: ENCOUNTERS WITH THE DEVIL AND HIS MINIONS, FALLEN ANGELS, and the POSSESSED edited by John Skipp. He collects antique straight razors and miles ridden on his bike.

ARTWORK

MIKE DUBISCH is an internationally known fantasy illustrator and graphic novelist. His art has been used in toy design and illustration for Star Wars and Dungeons & Dragons role playing games, covers for Aliens VS Predator, the graphic adaptation of Edgar Rice Burroughs' I AM A BARBARIAN, as well as appearances in the magazines SCIENCE FICTION AGE, REALMS OF FANTASY, THE H.P. LOVECRAFT MAGAZINE of HORROR, and THE CREEPS.

LOVECRAFT MEANS NEVER HAVING TO SAY YOU'RE SORRY
GOODFELLOW'S GUIDE TO THE OLD ONES

CODY GOODFELLOW has written five solo novels and two more with NY times bestselling author John Skipp. Two of his collections, SILENT WEAPONS FOR QUIET WARS and ALL-MONSTER ACTION, both received the Wonderland Book Award. He wrote, co-produced and scored the short Lovecraftian hygiene film STAY AT HOME DAD, which can be viewed on YouTube. As a bishop of the Esoteric Order of Dagon he presides over several Cthulhu Prayer Breakfasts each year. He is also a co-founder of Perilous Press, an occasional micropublisher of modern cosmic horror. He currently lives in Portland, OR.

WIDDERSHINS

EDWARD M. ERDELAC is the author of twelve novels including MONSTRUMFUHRER, ANDERSONVILLE, and THE MERKABAH RIDER series. His short stories have seen print in over two dozen anthologies and collections, including the Stoker Award winning After DEATH, OCCULT DETECTIVE QUARTERLY, and STAR WARS INSIDER MAGAZINE. Born in Indiana, educated in Chicago, he resides in the Los Angeles area with his family. News and excerpts from his work can be found at *emerdelac.wordpress.com*.

READY FLAYER ONE

SCOTT R JONES is a Canadian writer living in Victoria BC Canada with his wife and two frighteningly intelligent spawn. His stories have appeared in INNSMOUTH MAGAZINE, PSEUDOPOD, ANDROMEDA SPACEWAYS INFLIGHT MAGAZINE, and others. His first published story, TURBULENCE, received an Honorable Mention in CHIZINE'S IMAGINARIUM 3: BEST CANADIAN SPECULATIVE FICTION. Anthology appearances include CTHULHU FHTAGN! (Word Horde), FLESH LIKE SMOKE (April Moon Books), RETURN OF THE OLD ONES and THE CHILDREN OF GLA'AKI (both from Dark Regions Press) as well as ETERNAL FRANKENSTEIN (Word Horde). He's also the author of the non-fiction work WHEN THE STARS ARE RIGHT: TOWARDS AN AUTHENTIC R'LYEHIAN SPIRITUALITY (Martian MigrainePress) and the editor of the anthologies RESONATOR: NEW LOVECRAFTIAN TALES FROM BEYOND, CTHULHUSATTVA: TALES OF THE BLACK GNOSIS, A BREATH FROM THE SKY: UNUSUAL STORIES OF POSSESSION, and the upcoming CHTHONIC: WEIRD TALES OF INNER EARTH.

WE'LL KNOW THE REASON WHEN THE WORLD PARTS ITS LIPS

JESSICA MCHUGH is a novelist and internationally produced playwright running amok in the fields of horror, sci-fi, young adult, and wherever else her peculiar mind leads. She's had twenty-one books published in nine years, including her bizarro romp, THE GREEN KANGAROOS, her Post Mortem Press bestseller, RABBITS IN THE GARDEN, and her YA series, THE DARLA DECKER DIARIES. More information on her published and forthcoming fiction can be found at *JessicaMcHughBooks.com*.

SUJN'S LITTER

MATTHEW M. BARTLETT is the author of THE STAY-AWAKE MEN AND OTHER UNSTABLE ENTITIES, GATEWAYS TO ABOMINATION, CREEPING WAVES, and other books of supernatural horror. His short stories have appeared in a variety of anthologies, including LOST SIGNALS, A BREATH FROM THE SKY, YEAR'S BEST WEIRD FICTION VOL. 3, and DARKER COMPANIONS, a tribute to Ramsey Campbell. He lives in a small brick house on a quiet, leafy street with his wife Katie Saulnier and their cats Phoebe, Peachpie, and Larry.

THEY DELIGHT IN EXTINCTION

CHRISTOPHER SLATSKY'S stories have appeared in THE YEAR'S BEST WEIRD FICTION VOL. 3, NIGHTSCRIPT VOL. 2, LOOMING LOW, DARKER COMPANIONS, and elsewhere. His debut collection ALECTRYOMANCER AND OTHER WEIRD TALES was released summer of 2015. He currently resides in the Los Angeles area.

www.ingramcontent.com/pod-product-compliance
Lightning Source LLC
Chambersburg PA
CBHW080924190726
48293CB00010B/2675